Selected short stories (The first volume)

Gopal Patra

ISBN 978-93-5610-601-7
© Gopal Patra 2022
Published in India 2022 by Pencil

A brand of
One Point Six Technologies Pvt. Ltd.
123, Building J2, Shram Seva Premises,
Wadala Truck Terminal, Wadala (E)
Mumbai 400037, Maharashtra, INDIA
E connect@thepencilapp.com
W www.thepencilapp.com

DISCLAIMER: *This is a work of fiction. Names, characters, places, events and incidents are the products of the author's imagination. The opinions expressed in this book do not seek to reflect the views of the Publisher.*

Author biography

Gopal Patra: -

The life of a poet-storyteller is an invincible soldier who fought in battle - whose tool is fearlessness and honesty ... Search Google for details and type in Bengali or English letters. If you search "Gopal Patra" you will get all the information…

Address :-Gopal Patra
Vill- Bhagabati Pur
P.O - Chaturvuj kati
P.S - Shankrail
Dist- Howrah
Pin Cod - 711313
West Bengal - India
Mobile number9143098660
Email address:-patragopal561@gmail.com
Facebook link:-
 https://www.facebook.com/profile.php?

CONTENTS

Selected short stories
(The first volume)

Selected short stories
   (The first volume)
   Gopal Patra

Dedication:- All story loving people…

"Selected short stories"

Thiscollection of short stories of unique taste written over the last few years has found a place ...

Theseare just some of the stories my own timeline has received reviews for in various online magazines and groups.

Those stories are respectively...

1) " Half architect of love "
2) " Honey cycle "
3) " Guest "
4) " Chakravyuh "
5) " Invalid relationship "
6) " Migratory "

Fromthese stories you can get all the supplies of life. As the socio-economic aspects have been highlighted in it, so the love-love-hate and contempt and equally have blossomed.

Now, if my readers like it, then I will consider my work worthwhile.

Gopal Patra

Author's biography

Gopal Patra:- **The** life of an impeccable poet-storyteller, an invincible soldier who fought in the war - whose tool is fearlessness and honesty ... Search Google for details "Gopal Patra" Or "Gopal Patra" in English Search "Gopal Patra" and you will get all the information.

Table of contents

1) "Half Architect of Love"

2) "Honey Cycle"

3) "Guest"

" Half architect of love"

Chapter One

Boo- Boo- What happened today.

Sushant could not even dream that such a thing would happen ...

Aunty didn't see it but why did Tulii become so reckless ... Sushant can't think anymore! Lying in bed and fidgeting all night.

 The son of a very ordinary middle class family has just entered Calcutta University to complete his M.Sc. graduation.

Sushant used to stay with them before taking the Higher Secondary Examination.

 But Sushant is not eligible to leave. She has passed secondary school with 75% marks and high school with 80% marks, so .. despite the consent of her grandparents ... she has taken the helm of life in her own hands. Can't pay.

 So Sushant keeps her mother and keeps her expenses by doing five to ten tuitions ... but when the ghost of socio-economy is on her head, sometimes life seems to fail.

Tulika nickname "Tuli" is a first year student in B.A.

Tuli's father Anirban Dutt is the manager of a big office in Kolkata! It goes without saying that there is no shortage - big flat - car which is called affluent family! This is the only child of the parents ...

This very talented student reads this brush at home - Sushant comes to teach Bangla for a couple of hours in the evening three days a week ....

Sushant is teaching Tulika for two years now.

Chapter Two

Tuli'sfather Anirban Babu has been chosen as his daughter's teacher because of his good reputation as a good tutor in Bengal. Sushantar also loves .

Tuli's parents enough for amicable use ... pays off on time.

 But how will the relationship look like after the incident today?
Sushant can't think ...

 Tulika's mother is a very kind lady - she sees Sushant in her son's eyes! Good or bad, don't leave without eating something new ..

Sushant is very ashamed but Tulika sometimes has no choice but to start eating such a boy!
 Nowadays, this nuisance has increased a bit, Sushant has felt in his mind.

Tulika's mother calls Anila Devi aunty and the lady is very happy. Tulika's father discusses the details from time to time .. Besides, Sushant's chances of getting admission in Calcutta University have increased because of him! He looks at Sushant with good eyes ...

Heavy sweet girl Tulika looks and is very beautiful. Fifteen of the sixteen collars exist in her! She can easily feed two or five boys but Tuli is not like that ..

A little differently polite - humble but very smart ... She has a smile on her face.

Tulika doesn't like seeing Sushant as a tutor, but loves to look at her friend's eyes ...

feels more comfortable! So a lot of the time a lot of discussions come out of the study..Daily Stories-Sociology-Economics.

Then Tulika said .. Money tie all Sushantada?

Nothing beyond that?

I don't know if there is anything, but now the money is tied to the society.

Tulika looks a little sad ... she says I have all the money - money home - you can say car sometimes why very - very lonely? I think there is nothing at all.

I can't say that but if I had money I could have done better! I could have been better established in life! You don't understand the pain of poverty Tulika ... If my financial condition was good, I would have to come to your house today to study in a storm?

Sushant said the words that day out of excitement ...

No brush that day did not find any answer! Just saying in my mind Sushantada, if you understood my mind, you would not be able to say that! Sushant forgot to take the seven early side bag TO that he was not taught that day.

Chapter Three

Oneand a half days Tulika would ask me to read a magazine or a book of poems without opening the textbook or to explain the meaning of the poem ...

You understand all that well, I don't know, I don't understand, open the book and see if you have done home tax?

What else to do?

Like an injured deer, he opens his eyes and sits with his head down .... After a while .... Sushant says in a calm voice- where do you read?

But the brush sits like a frost ... Tell Sushant without getting any answer .... Let me see what is in your book. Tulika smiles and offers the book like an offering ... Sushant's eyebrows are wrinkled! This is "Vanusingh Tagore's words" love words ....

I say reading is all this is happening now .. I understand love? Tulika asks a question .. Tulika doesn't answer but just looks at Sushant's face with a cowardly cowardly look.

The obsession of feeling unbearably good is created between the two of them as if they have known each other for a long time. This is the first time that Sushant has kept an eye on a girl .... And in her mind she felt that girls are so beautiful. .. What a wonderful creation ...

After eye-to-eye like this for a while, with big eyes, smiling face, Tulika became the first to say, "Will you recite it ..."

Oi to ..... gahan kusumkunj-maje mildar madhur banshi baje ...

Cut off the feeling of indifference and shake the throat.

Sushant started first ... In the middle of the deep kusumakunja, there is a soft sweet flute,
Bisri tras-loklaje sajni, ao ao lo.
The limbs are blue,

The two of them fell in love ... Love in the heart,

Bimal smiles at the deer's eye, come to Kunjabanme.

Sushant: - Dhale Kusum Surabhavar, Dhale Bihag Surabasar,

Tulika: - Dhale Indu Amritdhar Bimal Rajat Bhati Re.
Evil evil beetle humming, a thousand kusum kunje kunje,

Sushant: - Futal Sajni, Punje Punje Bakul Yuthi Jati Re.
Look, Sajni, love overflows in Shyamra's eyes,
Madhur Bahasirdan Amritsadan is slandering the moon.

Together the two: - Aao aao sajanibrinda, herb sakhi srigobinda

Shyamco Padarbinda Bhanusingh has been arrested.

(The above part is taken from the essay titled Padabali of Vanusingh Tagore)

After reciting in a gurgling voice, the two of them burst out laughing like free birds ...

Laughter spreads all over the house - the heart of the soul - the soul spreads all over the heart .....

Chapter Four

Tulika'smother was standing behind the door with tea and snacks, the boy and the girl were hiding and watching the two shoots ... at first it was difficult but then it became easy - in my mind what is evil will make both of them quite happy ... and no father wants me to see the boy and girl happy.

He was glad to think of this ... so he opened the door a little and snorted .... Take a cup of tea and water ...

Tuli puts tea and snacks in front of Sushant ... So Sushant got up and said, "Where are you? I'm very hungry today ..."

Tulika Anjali offers the same snack in front of Sushant ...

Stunned by what he thought, Sushant swallowed a cup of tea ...

Then ... Never in the space of reading Tulika says let's go out a little or go to the veranda and stand for a while, what a sweet south wind is blowing.

Sushant said in a calm voice, what do you have to do now?

Don't have to read the test in front?

Tulika muttered silently in her mind, maybe this time I will go crazy.

How much more will I read in my mind that I want you, do you not understand or do not want to understand ....
That will be another day when I come here to take you for a walk?
Let's read ...

But to be honest, I think Sushant is very sad for Tulika ... thinking of Tilika ... but Tulika is the only girl in such a big house to be avoided - it is incongruous to have a close relationship with a normal M-read boy ... He realizes that Tulika loves him ... not that he doesn't love her too ..

I dream of having a house and a life partner like you .. but there is no way ...

But the mind can not always be fooled! How does Tulika deny love?

Tulika sits using a day or two that has no real basis.
It was Sushant's birthday that day, so Anila Devi invited Sushant for dinner - but she could not keep the invitation!
..

So he ignored his mother's request and came home ...

The next day, as usual, when I went to teach tuition, I met Tuli's mother for the first time.

Sushantar's chest heaved when he heard the words. He said in a worried voice, "Let's go and see what happened."

Anila Devi continued to say in a worried but calm voice, "I don't know what happens to a girl who is always like that..

Aunt Sushanta, don't worry so much! Everything will be fine. Bring food. I will feed you. See if you can feed Dad .. I go Sushant switched on as soon as he entered the house .. The whole house was flooded with light and Tulika looked up ...

What are you doing?
Tulika tried to hide something by turning off the light - no answer.

Sushant sat down beside the bed and said in a consoling voice ..... What are you starting boyish?
Why haven't you eaten since yesterday?
  Aunt Mesomshai, what do you think?

You are making a mistake. I promised Tulika's mother, so I could not keep your request.

Tulika called her eyes with her hand and said in a soft voice. I can spend a day fasting and swearing .. Can you just Sushant Da? It will never happen again ...

Tulika looked up at Sushant The gaze of the gaze goes deeper and deeper .... From then on, despite her reluctance, Tulika had to protect Sushant ...

Chapter Five

Inthis way, how many unjust desires have been met by Sushant. She is now a second year student Sushant's A-May result is good.

It went on like this ... but what happened today is not normal Today I was caught by two people ... my mind was tied ...

Today, Sushant's body was not good, coughing with fever! But Tulika has to go to school - she didn't go to college today - so Bella Belly came to study ...

Sushant got out of the house at four o'clock with this thought in her head! As soon as Aniladevi saw Sushant arriving at Tuli's house at 4.30 pm, she said, "Daddy, is it so early today?"

I don't mean the body is not good - that's why I thought ... Sushant said the words mumbling! Getting vocal -

Where did the lightning come from? Mind and body will be all right ... Even though I wanted to, Sushant's head was going to be cut off in front of my aunt - what would he think of such a thing!

But the result is just the opposite. Come on, but ....
But I will return very soon, said Sushant.
Tulika is standing on one leg .... she gets dressed quickly ...

she told her mother that she is coming then ..

Yeah Al that sounds pretty crap to me, Looks like BT aint for me either.

After walking side by side for a while, it seemed as if the master with three students seemed to be incompatible ...

So the taxi called Sushant reached in five to ten minutes ... by the river.

Tulika walks along the river bank for a while as if she can't say anything .. her lips are trembling .. she seems to be indifferent- Sushant looks anxious!

After walking for a while, I don't like Sushant. Let's sit on that grass for a while, so let's go home ... on the grass! The two sit side by side Sushant looks up at the sky ...

The sun was setting then, and it was as beautiful as the bride's vermilion tip ...

Draw a picture in the western sky as if immersed in its own game ...

Applying colors to the canvas and changing the mind again! Birds are flying in flocks ....
The sun is sinking then red like the tip of the bride's vermilion ....

Draw a picture in the western sky as if immersed in its own game ...

Applying colors to the canvas and changing the mind again! Birds are flying in flocks!
 Seeing all these sailing boats floating in the river, Sushant seemed to be distracted .. Suddenly he was startled ..

Tuli raised her hand and showed Sushant that she saw two colorful butterflies flying over the river in a strange way ...

 They both deal with their confidence as they choose to embark on their play activities.

Tulika said, "Mother, how dare you ..." Sushant laughed just like you! Can't you be that brave too Sushantada?
The two of them were silent for a while ...
Tulika pointed to the sky again ...

Sushant saw two birds fluttering in the sky .... Sushant looked at Tulika and said- you can fly like that like a bird ..
Tulika's clear answer, if you are by my side, I can do everything ... everything ...
Sushant said with a soft smile, but it will happen .. but let's get up today.

 After a while, when the two of them reached home, Tuli's mother said, "Why did you come back so early, Eli?"
 No, I don't think so ...

I was saying that the body is not good, so I was saying that I would not have read today! But are you showing the doctor?

Not a little fever and you will be cured! Look, don't tie anything again.

Mother, you sit in the study room .... I am arranging tea and snacks ..

All these conversations ended in one fell swoop and Aniladevi said goodbye.

But surprisingly, Tulika didn't say anything since then.
She agreed to her mother's words, shaking her head ... Both of them go and sit in the reading room ....

Now take out the book .. Tulika opens the book but the open book is still read ... Sushantar looks at it mysteriously.

Before he could see the fire in Fagun's eyes or the sun before seeing the bride ...

Tulika jumps on Sushant like a ferocious tiger, hugs her and starts kissing her ...

A-mi-o to-ma-ke bhishan ..va.lo.ba.c .. Su-sha-nt fills the whole room with frequent breathing ... The mind and the whole body get wet ...
At that time load shedding ... Who knows how long it has been like this .. Suddenly the two of them startled at the sound of mother's voice - He kept saying from the kitchen that Tulika tea has become cold ...

Who knows when the light is on ...

Tulika goes out ... with a lot of fascination Tea - When you come back with a snack and see the brush, it's just a void ....

 Probably not..

" Honey cycle"

(The story of a decaying society)

Agovernment NGO went missing while trying to gather information on sexual health. Then the hands of various brokers turned to the city of Mumbai The story of a girl who was sold to one of the many conventional brothels.

There is no caste - religion and no lower or upper age for girls of almost all ages Village - Ganj - City - Suburbs are disappearing at noon every day ...

Women abduction - Women trafficking rings have become very active lately- The beehive has sprung up all over the city.

Our country, India, has become a huge industry for abducting women and trafficking women all over the world.

In this cycle, people from almost all walks of life, including leaders, bureaucrats, singers, singers and actors are left out.

And all these incidents are happening at the tip of the administration's nose - the role of Dhritarashtra has come down despite the administration knowing everything.

Trafficking in women abduction of women ... torture of women পরিণত has become a major disease of a society.

But it seems to be a passive part of the larger section of society. On the contrary, the girl of that family is the victim of this disgusting situation Contempt for the girl's family .. busy throwing hatred.

But is there any way to cure this social disorder?

There is a little courage in the Boiki administration to do a little work-mindedness - and this disorder can be easily overcome if they have dedication and sense of duty towards their work.

In the midst of so much darkness, the direction of a little light is a brave and fearless police officer Miss Devarati Sen ...

Women have the highest power - different scriptures say that.

That is the proof in this story. Only a brave woman is able to find Path of Light - The path to women's liberation.

Chapter One

Ayeshasuddenly met his eyes with a soft voice with an impossible growl. Where is he now?
 She is lying half naked in a huge bed! Tried to lift the head but unbearable pain all over the body as if the veins of the head are tearing! Tried again and again but could not get up! Trying to feel with the seven senses of the body, he could remember that ..

 Like any other day, he went to people's houses to collect information on his own NGO.

As soon as he stood in front of a palace-proof house, a young man like a prince welcomed him inside the house and gave him a glass of cold drink! I do not remember anything about the diameter!

 Where is his address now?
Through whom did he come here?

Nothing comes to mind! Feeling we have 'Run out of gas' emotionally because of the pain in the middle of the thighs.

Maybe it's a big hotel or brothel where the animals have been eating his meat for days ...
 It is not possible to think or feel anything else as if the wires of the head are tearing ...

the awakening of unconsciousness! In this situation, TE suddenly saw someone with a needle in his hand ... After a while he became unconscious ....!

Chapter Two

Whois this Ayesha? Ayesha, daughter of a lower middle class Muslim family?

Pushing Guje passed high school ...
Not bad to see.

The condition of the father's emergency work is not good .. It is not possible for the father alone to take care of the stomach of three brothers ...

That is why Ayesha chose her job as an NG of a very small month! Going from house to house to collect various information,.

Ayesha went to Nawabganj on the same day ... then disaster ...

Has anything happened to the police?

Missing diary has been kept at Nawabganj police station from home ... N, G, is doing its best but it has been almost a week since the police could not find any information.

So did an eighteen-nineteen year old girl suddenly disappear in Bharadupura?

Going to the police, the father had to be harassed again and again! The police said --- Look, your daughter has fallen in love with someone ...

I mean there was love-trem? Find out ... Don't bother us unnecessarily ... you know we have a lot of important work to do! I will definitely let you know when I get the news that the police are doing the work of the police.

Such a body image of the police?
But who will solve the problem?
That path is in the rock 7.

A group of different speaking girls whispered and Ayesha woke up yesterday and met her eyes.

I don't understand what they are saying. I just realized that they are saying .. new bird
And laughing among themselves .. Some are peeking into the house.

At that time, a middle-aged woman entered his house and mixed Hindi and Bengali, which is what he meant by this ...

Ayesha noticed new clothes with perfume oil soap in her hand! He sat down next to her bed and stopped laughing to give a little scolding to the girls who were peeping ...

Get up Betty ... this is your house today ...

Ayesha tried to get out of bed, her body ached a little ... her head was a little heavy! He said softly, "Where am I?"

You are now the biggest Tinkuvai in Mumbai ...
It is not difficult for Ayesha to understand that she has been sold to a famous brothel in Mumbai in a few days.

The lady again said in Hindi-Bangla combination .. Tinku bhai ne apko five lakh ki nagad kharidi ho ... uhar hukum toke saaf sutar - paricharya kara hamar kam ... tonight another babu go saat tinku vivi aste kare!

Khabardar betiya and lok baner sher se khatranak ... usko khush kar dena chahiya!
Tera unko pasand hoga to samajalo barat khul gaya aur pasand nehi hoga to aapke haddia aur mas kutta khayenge ...

Ayesha's bed aunt rubbed oil on her hair and scratched it.

Hearing this, Ayesha's whole body and mind were shrinking .. Today there is going to be another auction here.
Aunty continues to say that all the old things are wrong, son ...

She has no plants ...

Aunty's eyes were filled with tears and two drops of tears fell on Ayesha.

Aromatic oils - Soaps, nice baths and new clothes ... Eating and drinking at noon is good! Seeing all this, Ayesha was remembering the sacrificial animal- Helpless, he had to do everything like a wooden doll.

Chapter Three

Theevening came .. Aunty and the other two girls arranged her and took her to a tidy room,.

When night falls, a living ghost enters the house ... a living gin ... whose picture is seen on the page of a boy ...

On the one hand, the face is dazzling, on the other hand, the big black eyes are blind again ... as if saliva is dripping from the tongue to eat meat ...

What a horrible Ayesha got up and closed her eyes when she saw the image.

The living human skeleton suddenly said yes Hamii ... Tinku Bhai ... Tinku -... Tinku Bhai ...

The room was filled with vampire laughter ...
He stopped laughing and said .. Ayesha Bibi, let's relax for a while.

After giving five lakh rupees in cash, you today ha ... mother ...! Yes yes yes ...

Immediately took possession of the bed ....
Open the veil, Ayesha Bibi, you will be our queen ...

Ayesha is closing her eyes, as if someone suddenly said ... I don't like you, you will be bitten by a dog for a month ...!

That beginning ... Then darkness and darkness ... Who knows how many unfortunate women like her spend their days in darkness like this day after day ... Is there no way out of this darkness?

In Nawabganj, two or three more cases of disappearance have occurred in the last two to three months! Forty-year-old sari-blouse seller, a woman and a nineteen-twenty-year-old seller at Water Purifier ...

Naturally Nawabganj has created an atmosphere of panic! Which giant arrived in Nawabganj? One of the day is going to be an example of a living girl? It was not like that before.

And the police can not do any edge! How is it That is why the people and the opposition political party are coming under pressure from all around Continuous ... And things are happening in the same way in one and a half kilometers ...

It must have a rule ...!

Chapter Four

Forall these anti-social activities An officer from Special Branch has been sent in charge of Nawabganj Police Station ....
Miss Devarati Sen ...

He won as a general police officer due to lack of money ...

But due to his bravery and intelligence, a special officer of the crime branch of the police has been appointed in a short time.
Datale in West Bengal - that drug cycle Chakra was caught in the news .. He had a major role in it .

With the charge of Nawabganj in hand, he sat down with all the senior officers for the purpose of getting the edge of the shore ...
Mr. Das ... Ayesha means Ayesha Khatun's missing case in your hands? How far? It's been about six months ...

No, ma'am ... I haven't gone far ... Do you understand how difficult it is to catch an unnamed criminal?

Mr. Das mumbled ....
Yeah Al that sounds pretty crap to me, Looks like BT aint for me either.

I don't mean ...

You mean, like, saltines and their ilk, eh? From today, read Adajal ...

Mr. Sharma, isn't your mother a blacksmith? Is it the edge of Kaddur?

Gee mam ... to be honest I did an investigation for a while ... she thought mommy goddess was selling sari-blouse from which house she went missing but we couldn't find it even after investigation madam.

The area is so crowded ... Moreover, as a result of being a factory, people of different castes and religions live in rented flats.

I did not like your safa Mr. Sharma! Ok i gave you time too stick

Gee mam ...

And Mr. Chakraborty, your Dolan Roy water purifier seller ... is nineteen or twenty! What happened to its edges?

The events of last month have not yet been investigated under the pressure of other work, ma'am…

What is the stress of such work? As far as I know, Nawabganj is a peaceful area .. A few disappearances have started. In the last few months, the people of the political party seem to be quite peaceful.

Didn't get the time or did it on purpose?
No, madam, are you right?

But I'm going to go a little further ... like that I faced a hurdle What more can I say?

Tied up ... then you will get some news from your stomach - OK we can sit down and discuss with you later.

Everybody listen with open minds ... there are three missing persons ... they all but serve the people ... some collect information .. some sell goods .... right

Almost everyone present said in unison
Yes mam ... right ...

That means they go from house to house or flat ... Missing from home or flat.

From the roadside or elsewhere but not ...
That means any house or flat in the area The secret of their disappearance is hidden?
Do you agree with me?

Maybe ma'am ... maybe ... Almost everyone said in unison.

Then why sit and look in every house or flat ... then the house that is suspected Make her list!
I want a preliminary report within 15 days. Anyone who needs help will get everything.

So far today .....
Good night ... al
l the best ...

Chapter Five

S,PMr. Majumder K Debarti A company is recruiting additional police and the work is progressing very fast ...

Every day one or the other house is being raided at an inopportune time.

In these days, ten suspects have been identified in the house or flat.

Of these, Bedarti has given a list of three very suspicious people in different formulas ...

He raided two houses for two days in a row but did not find any clues or good answers ... and only one flat remained .... Block-B Room Number Thirteen ...

The only resident is Anarul Mollah ...
And faith is the secret of this disappearance in that flat! So all the work is already done.

A conspiracy has been hatched by the police to trap the criminals?

Of course, in all the plans Debarati Devi ... there has been some disagreement with the senior officers about this ...
but after explaining with logic, everyone has accepted her words! Someone said .. are you going to be a little ricks

mam?

Maybe ... What happens if you are afraid of the police? Besides, you are in danger, don't you all jump to save this little sister?

Definitely ... Definitely .. Everyone said in unison ...

So what is fear? In time, all will be revealed!
Time 10 am Block-B-Room Number Thirteen Calling Sand Hand ...

Hrithik Roshan Sulabh, a young man of twenty-five or twenty-six years old, came out from inside with two or three tungtang sounds and saw a woman of nineteen or twenty years waiting ...

The young man asked - what's the matter?
The woman said - Seven creams - perfume - scent Need something, sir?

If you want to see our products ...
please import all the products please see?

Oh yes of course?
I prefer foreign things .. come on ... Come in.

O sir .... thank you sir ... thank you ...

He kept the young man and woman inside the room and closed the door well.

He showed a sofa inside the room and asked the girl to sit down and asked her to put the bag on the table.
The young lady does that ... and says thank you so much ...

So my product shows you? Are there no more people in your house?
I mean, if they had seen me I would have had more product sales ...

No madam I live flat alone ... but no worries about your product sale- if you like I will buy all the products! And the whole cash in hand ...

Thank you very much ...

That's right madam What do you eat before you see the product?
Have you traveled so far?
Tea-coffee or cold drinks?
Then the good is not bad?

All right, wait a minute, I'll bring it from above ....

Orange juice came in a glass ... Orange juice ... Please eat.

Thanks ... Your hospitality is very nice.

All the blessings of God - I do a little bit, madam.

Take it, madam, you can eat it. No, it will take more time, just five minutes.

Please sir ...

After the young man went upstairs, the young woman eagerly filled a glass drink into a bottle and ran it through the bag.

And the young man is talking to someone else in a very soft voice.

Yes, in more than nine, five or seven minutes, the young man came and saw the empty glass and said excitedly How did the foot juice, madam?

Very nice ...

Now I will see all your products ...

What is it that madam is sitting like that?

Show your foreign products ...

Keep laughing
He unzipped the bag, pulled out the pistol, aimed it at Anirul's forehead and said loudly. Harry the baby pig ...
I will show you all my products .... Your game is over!

The criminal could not think what to do after eating Vyabachaka ...
Immediately some police officers came at the speed of an arrow and tied him up.

Remember me, Miss Debarati Sen, the baby pig - for the

Special Crime Branch ...

How many girls products You see, I will show you the product one by one,

Mr. Sen, do a good search of the flat, the documents will surely be found! And Mr. Sharma, you lock it up.

Searching the whole fat, a few SIM cards, a few mobile phones, all the documents that have been matched this time is a matter of wonder! Visa passport of different countries, pictorial identity card of different names of the same person ... Proof of all these is a large scale criminal?

SP needs to call Mr. Majumdar .. Hello sir ... I am Debarati.

Kindly if you come once

Wow, what could be bigger good news?
Congress My Boy ...

Sincere thanks sir ...

All right, I'm coming ..
. OK
Ok bye…

Chapter Six

Someplace media people have gathered outside the flat till then and who is harassing Debarati with various questions?

He just said that a panda of the beehive has been caught then what to say in the press meeting.

It's as if a worm has suddenly come out to dig a worm - that's it ... As the investigation progresses, the screen is leaking one by one! No one from the local leader to the big minister is left out in this cycle.

This is a very big international cycle of trafficking women! Not just in India ... their business in the USA ... even in England and Japan ...

A branch organization is located in the capital of almost every state! From those organizations - on the bus to the train - job advertisements are given with phone numbers in different places.

Seeing those notifications, educated boys and girls come looking for jobs .... Most of the educated girls are trafficked abroad by showing the temptation of higher jobs! In some cases, it is used directly in the hospital or in making banned blue-film.

Some handsome boys are trained to trap girls in love

... With their big money, they are living in all parts of the city. Bring a girl in the net of love and bring her to the flat and gain success by making her unconscious.

Or the temptation to run away and get married and sell it to a prostitute in Vine State through that company.

After doing two or three such haircuts in one place, the handsome boy's group left the city under another name and settled in another city ...

What is the form of their earnings? Good but they have a lot of big and small brokers step by step ...

Maybe the first step is one lakh then it will continue to decrease as much as it goes up! Like other products, prices fluctuate with age There is a difference ...

The price also depends on which product is being exported to which country ...

Nowhere else in the world to see such a business?

No investment, just earn ...

So this is the countrymen like India Is it any wonder that business will lean? The country where corruption is at its peak ...

So jhake-jhake, pale-pale who will be left out? The village is being deserted to choose the thug.

So Miss Debarati Sen has been threatened many times! The miscreants once dropped bombs on his car but by the grace of God he is alive.

S, P Mr. Majumdar called the district governor and kept two commanders as his bodyguards! Twenty-four hours to place police pickets in his house.

But there is a place of trust with the people and the media! In these news, the politics of the state and the country has become turbulent.

However, some intellectuals think that nothing has happened except the body - this is the way of thinking ...

As the investigation progresses, the names of one actor-actress-singer-singer-VIP leader-minister are coming up one after another ....
In this honeycomb ...

In the case of the state, the CID center The CBI has taken charge of the investigation!

Since this beehive is international, the cooperation of the Foreign Minister and the Foreign Ministry is absolutely necessary to negotiate with other countries at the ministry level.

Debarati does not know when this investigation will end? Will everyone extend a helping hand?

Because from birth he has seen the majority win in the end.

Going to remove the twist of society Wouldn't he himself become a minority?

I left this question mark to people of all levels.

" Guest"

The story of a lonely man.

Chapter One

Whattime is it then? It will be a quarter to ten - at that moment a car came and stopped at the sound of a bell ringing ...
Maybe Sushovan Babu was waiting for this auspicious moment.

Busy opening the door ...

That's when Eli but so late that mother?
Do you know how much trouble the father is in the world pohate! Besides, you have grandchildren to tell them - it's a little late, Dad! The stranger mumbled and said with some surprise ...

Come on mom, come on mom, don't be late ...
They both entered the room.

Wow: I see all ready, Dad?

Also tell me what is the way? Collected all online - cakes - candles - and your favorite polao - royal kebabs everything ...

If you had a mother, she would do all that - I wouldn't have any trouble! See how the cake is. You always like chocolate, so ...

Wow... excellent -very nice ..

Dad is very beautiful! I like your answer.

After checking the health of Sushovan Babu's body, Neeli said - Dad, this year you set foot in seventy-five - I'm right ..?

Yes, my child Can't believe it?

Not exactly, father - the impression of age has not yet been so! You're really young now ...

Thank you very much but Do you think I should get out of bed with my pants on?

Dad, why are you going to think that?

"Oh my young lady. I am a big army man ... I have struggled so much and I am still going on ...

Talk about rubbing salt in my wounds - d'oh! It's not too late, my boy .... Let's start cutting the cake ...

All right - so be it ... Yeah Al that sounds pretty crap to me, Looks like BT aint for me either

Bata nevao - nevao - bah Let's start cutting the cake ...

Happy Birthday to you ... Happy Birthday to my dear Daddy ... Happy Birthday to you ...

Sushovan Babu feeds a piece of cake to Nili and puts it on his forehead. Nili does the same ...

Chapter Two

WhenI was a kid, I used to have a lot of trouble with your grandfather on my birthday cake ...

Once in the corner of the table to rush Your lips were cut off then she cried - do you remember?

Sushovan hugs Babu tightly - I don't remember that again.

Throat mother - can I still endure so much stress like then? How old are you?
I will not leave - close your eyes first ... I understand ...

With a small packet of decorative hands - Now open your eyes ...

What's so significant about a goat's head? "

This is a gift for my birthday boy ...

Why did you go to do all this again? B: Dad's birthday daughter has to come empty handed or not?

I will never be able to get along with you - let's do something, give a little of my favorite drink bottle from the fridge - and put all the food on the table ...

So let's talk while eating ...

This is your favorite drink, a bottle of wine
Dad still can't leave it.

I have given up everything, mother, I have become
destitute after leaving ... Now I have read some good
books and sometimes a little ...

Where is the food? Dad ... I want to hear a lot of stories
and recitations from you now!
That's fine - let's just say I've had a hard time ...
Sushovan Babu drinks two pots in a row and holds a
cigarette ...

Where did I put my cigarette hair again?
The one in front of you -
Where?

Don't open the packet, Dad ...

Oh mad, then you have brought your father's favorite
object!

I do not understand that your daughter likes and dislikes
you? Let's start the story this time ...

But where to start?
When I understand the eyes, a lot of memories come to
my mind- I am wondering which one to say and which one
to omit ...

Don't do one thing, start the day with the first
conversation with mom ...

Chapter Three

Thatday was our college freshman ... I am reciting loudly on stage ...

My favorite poet "Poems of Jibananda Das Banalta Sen "

For thousands of years I have walked the path of the earth,
From the Sinhala Sea to the Malay Sea in the dark of night I've been around a lot; In the gray world of Ashoka of Bhimsa I was there; In the darker city of Vidarbha; I am a weary soul, the sea of life around me, Bonalata Sen of Natore gave me two bars of peace.
Her hair is the nightmare of her dark side, Th face is the artwork of his Sravasti; After the sea The sailor who broke the hull lost direction When he sees the land of green grass inside the Cinnamon Island, I saw it in the dark; He said, "Where have you been all this time?" Natore's wildness Sen raised his eyes like a bird's nest.
Like the sound of dew at the end of all days Evening comes; The wings have been shown solely to give a sense of proportion. When all the colors of the world are extinguished, the manuscript is arranged Then the colors of the fireflies flickered in the story; All the birds come into the house — all the rivers — all the transactions of this life in Fura; There is only darkness, the savagery of sitting face to face.

Then ...

Then when I got off the stage, many of my admirers signed autographs I opened the notebook or diary to get it - one of them was standing behind me to get a hand ...

I put my hand in his and looked at his face in amazement - what can I say to you ... Really- her hair is the night of her dark side, The face is the art of her sravasti ...

This is my true wildness! Sinhala is not the sea - not in the darkness of the night or in the Malay Sea ...

I have not been able to find my wildness on my college campus so far .... Then ...

Then, touching her soft flower-like hand for a while, I looked at her face in amazement. In his gentle rebuke.

Can't I get an autograph because Mister takes my good diary?

When I got back to Sambit, I said yes, of course - but I didn't know what to write.
"You are my savagery. Sushovan ...
Seeing this, he blushed in shame. Sucharita said goodbye with a sweet smile like that day!
Then ....

The first meeting that day then - friendship ... gradually the friendship deepened and turned into love! Walking together ...
Eating and drinking together in the canteen ... college cut movies ... Then .... After finishing my studies, I got a job in

the army - then what a happy marriage ...

 First your grandfather then you Eli lighted my house ...
Grandpa went abroad as a big computer engineer and never came back ...
And you went to my husband's house far away Mumbai.

 And seeing you, your Mao went to the land of no return one day! Now I ... Alone Alone ..

Chapter Four

Ilooked at the clock hanging on the wall. And it will not be too late.

So hurry up .. But I have no shortage of money bank balance Tell me, Bharati Devi, how can you be alone in such a big house?

To break this loneliness I contracted you for two hours on my birthday ...

And you are very intelligent- Because you didn't have to teach me anything in advance, in one word you hinted that you played the role of my daughter till the end! Excellent Your Performance -

Not once in these two hours did you feel like Bharati Devi really took my daughter! This day will be remembered forever ...

This time you have to get up, right?

Your remuneration is inside this envelope!
Bharati Devi looked at Sushovan Babu and started thinking ... And he saw the old man twinkling in the corner of his eye ...

Honestly, she didn't even think for a second that she was a call girl.

Gives away his body for a fair wage - he has to change hands every night ...

Crowds gather to eat honey ... Bile burns when he sees an old customer ...

But he is helpless - forced to accept because the customer is his goal ...

Even today he was thinking of something like this ... Today it seems as if he is carrying a small cigarette case in his hand! Sometimes he takes small gifts for the customer and his purpose is nothing but to make the customer happy and get more money. ...

But every time Sushovan Babu opens the door and says, "Why are you so late, Mother Eli?"
This is the unique experience of his life ... the unique honor.

What do you think Bharati Devi? Open the envelope and see if it is OK. I will give it if it takes more .. I am very satisfied with you ...
Leave it to you Sushovan Babu .... Why?

At the bar I'm your daughter ... Can a daughter pay her father? Don't have to take?

If I change my mind about you in a blink of an eye, mother ... then so be it! But promise mother - Will I ever come to this old father?
Dad will tell you to come - and the girl will not come, is it

ever? I will definitely come (bowing) then come ...

Reaching the door ... Come, mother, come, but when it comes, bring it with my grandchildren, but ...

Well - I'll try, Dad ... Bharati Devi said the words with the car start! Sushovan Babu- He looks anxiously at the way ....

" Chakravyuh"

Torture is a symbol of women's rights.

Chapter One

Scene: -1

Openspace Pathghat Shunshan Bangla Patan house...
Veranda surrounded by bahari trees!

A BMW car came and stopped in front of the gate!
Suited-booted gentleman ...
As soon as he got down, a young woman came out with
her hands on the calling sand - they went inside together...

Scene2: -

Thebed room glistening with the light of the neon lamp,
the young woman leaned her body on the young woman's
body - Peg filled wine.

Scene3: -

Dreamblue   light. Side   by   side Up-down Bottom-
up. Young men and women.

Scene4: -

Lastnight - only two hands were seen. One hand is giving
a few taka notes and the other hand is taking the notes
with utmost care.

Scene5: -

Carstart. Let the birds fly!
****

Chapter Two

Scene1: -
Thewife of the BMW owner is waiting for her husband to return.

The front door is opened and the body, mind and understanding ...

It will be ten o'clock at ten o'clock ... maybe some surprise is waiting for him today - their first wedding anniversary ...

Scene2: -
Self-cooked menu of favorite water ... Disappointment with increasing night - Dark and crowded in the depths of the mind ...

Scene3: -
Suddenlyin the middle of the night I woke up in a nightmare .. It was twenty-three on the ticking clock! The bed is empty ... empty.
Her house is really on fire - along with her forehead and ...

Scene4: -
Thefront door is still open .... Anxiety is not one of the eyelids! Is there any serious danger?
The birds all roared at night ...
As usual, the hyacinth tree spreads light on the front door with the smell and ...

Scene5: -

Intensecity of BMW car .... Shiuli's chest wound - Calling sand hand-

What are you doing? You see - forget me in less than a year - Divya is asleep!

****

Chapter Three

Scene1: -

Themother of the girl who fell on the body of the young man is lying next to her six-year-old grandson. But nothing can calm him down! Where is the mother from time to time?

I'll go to Maar.

Do you know what the father does to his daughter?

If you say - mother you are old-fashioned - you do not know nowadays in the city day and night are equal! Car-horse-human work-action goes in equal rhythm! Does everyone get a good job during the day mom? Don't worry, just look at Piku - I'll take care of everything ...

Scene2: -

Really, if Urmi was not there, what would he do?

What happened to them?

Thinking about it ... the pillow gets wet with tears, mother!

This is how day goes - night goes - year goes by ...

Scene3: -

Itwas not wrong to recognize Anirban on that first day. Cheating on each other ... Even after getting married, the nature has not changed yet - I will make a situation that he can't even dream of! Seven years of revenge ...

Can't recognize him that day .... So Anirban is told to wait - and another pooch was painted on his face .... And bahari

- open fair dress ... needless to say.

Scene4: -

Somore .. Urmi keeps drunk on the sidewalk side by side ... Foss came out of Anirban's mouth. Today is my wedding anniversary. I have to go home!

He hugged her very close and said to Anirban, "I don't remember Babu, do you understand?" Your wife understands and she is lascivious - enchanting - better place than me?
Anirban said in an annoyed face, not all those issues!
But still the rest of the night ...

Scene5: -

Andthat day Anirban was throwing a whole bundle of five hundred rupees .... Urmi puts the money on his forehead and then says will Anirban Babu come again?

Of course you filled me up overnight ... can't come to you? He is my kindness babusab .... Thanks Ginger ... Goodbye If Urmi has worked in medicine in his mind?
****

Chapter Four

Scene1: -

It'sas if the state of intoxication is endless ... Every day he comes and goes to the Blue Moon Hotel.

He doesn't want anyone but Urmi ...! Only Urmi in his life now ... first and foremost!
Urmi will come to his time again untimely?
This is like the intoxication of hero-in Is that really so?

Little by little every day has made him accustomed to this drug!
Urmi smiles in revenge ... So the taste will be fulfilled today?
That video recording of all his and Anirban's feats has been done long ago ...

Scene2: -

Meanwhile, Anirban's chaste wife no longer waits for him! The doors of the mind including the front door and closed. How long can you wait? Wood that dries the mind and body!
So just a miscellaneous ... Somen from the flat next door comes and fills her with the gaps in her bed - soaking her mind and body!
And to see her full womb one day ...

Scene3: -

Noneed to break the pot in the market this time .. So

Urmi has already made all the arrangements ... Media - Press Everything ...

Extinguished in a timely manner ... Seeing Urmi silently, Anirban said..why darling is in so much mood? What happened?

The body is a little bad ...

What does that mean?

I mean, I'm going to be the mother of your baby ...

If you smile ... I come to this whore house to have fun in exchange for a handful of money! Not to be the father of the child ....

Anirban is laughing ...

Laughter is all around ...

Urmi then jumped like a ferocious tiger and grabbed Anirban's collar and said ... You don't recognize me baby pig?

Who plays a good home one day ... After enjoying it, you threw it in the sewer ....! Then you stood in the election and became a minister today, didn't you?

Think about it, was there anyone in your life called Malvika? And I am still alive to take revenge and I have saved your son too!

Hearing your journey to this hotel, I started this heinous act ...

In the meantime, when the people of the press and the media come together ... what they have started.

Scene4: -

FinanceMinister Anirban Mitra's Kechcha on almost every channel .... showing past activities fluently ... The front row dailies are also being printed in the newspapers on a regular basis ...

All the people are mad ....
Opposition groups called for the beleagured PM to resign.

Fifthandlastscene: -

Anirbanhas never been expelled from the post of minister .. now it is time to get in his way ...
Meanwhile, Urmi has received another receipt ..
That is what has been proved in court today The child is born of Piku Anirban ...

Finished .....

" Invalid relationship"

Chapter One

What'sthis? There is not a single thread to wear ... Covered in a thin velvet sheet, two bodies- Unconscious Vikram Babu sleeping in the same condition as him ...

But where is the clothing?
How to get up?
Enough intelligence or age to understand what happened to him at night- Manisha stepped on Baishe yesterday ...!

But Manisha tries to figure out what was used with her yesterday ...

Manisha's office boss means Vikram Babu - always a little weak towards her ...

As soon as he reached the office today, he made an urgent call and said - Manisha Not your birthday darling today - I'll give you a surprise after the holidays!

It is not possible to say boss face to face, so the two of them got into the boss's car and got up at the famous hotel "Blue-Moon" in the city.
Arriving at the hotel room, Manisha was not surprised to hear someone say -

Spacious hotel room - neatly arranged for a birthday party

... even the cake wax lamp is ready - but the guest is just a Vikram Babu ...
Do you like the room tidy?

Why did you go to do all this again?

Hey, I won't. You're my personal assistant. I won't celebrate your birthday. What's the matter?

After cutting the cake and lighting the lamp Gave a box of gifts - jewelry will be something!

Please do not open now! Let's have some light water and a little gossip - then what do you say the moment you can eat dinner?

Manisha shakes her head and agrees ... The hotel boy went with the bottle of drink on time as per the order ....

Vikram Babu made two pegs for two ... Manisha ...

Nao very light drink will not be a problem, the two of them poured Chias throat.

This is not Manisha's first time, but after eating a peg, to tell the truth, what kind of love is created - so at the request of the boss, he swallowed two more pegs in a moment!
It is as if his head is shaking ... He stood up and saw that his legs were shaking but all these sorrows and pains seemed to disappear in an instant ... Manisha wanted to fly like a bird.

So the two hands meet and pose like a flying bird Manisha is moving from side to side of the hotel room ...

What did Vikram feed him as soon as he came to him?
Sir, I feel very good - very good ...
And maybe for this moment Vikram is so organized!

Without a moment's delay, Vikram hugged Manisha and turned her around in a few twists and turns - the tide of blood began to flow all over her body! The mind wanted to sink into the abyss -

He wanted to eat a lot of caress so he hugged Vikram's neck more tightly.

Manisha's condition is like a goat cut in a well-made bed ... So it is not too late, Vikram jumps completely naked and ready for battle - just like a lion jumps on his favorite deer!

One by one, like an onion peel, he began to undress Manisha's body - with all his strength!
Storms all over the body - Wounded but no bleeding ...
Just floating in the sea of happiness - An unearthly joy - I hope nothing more - I want more - Manisha starts making indistinct voices ....

Chapter Two

Aftertaking a bath in the hotel room, the two of them sat face to face, refreshed.

Manisha opened the presentation box and was not only surprised but also surprised to find a gold necklace set with a diamond ...
What do you like?

Vikram smiled and said Vikram - Come closer and put your hand on your hand ...

Wearing Manisha's necklace, Vikram said to her ear, "I enjoyed it very much yesterday. You are a perfect match with my body. You are a perfect fit. And you have to appreciate your hunger too!"

Manisha said that day because of Vikram's voice and that is why I understand.
Yes, that's right ...

Vikram said, "You don't have to go to the office today. I will drive you to the flat. Then I will come to the office once. There is an urgent meeting."

That first. Since then, Manisha has spent various nights in different famous hotels in different states with Vikram in various office work.

No, Vikram doesn't have to resort to deception anymore. He has broken the barrier of shame and humiliation. He thinks that sex is a normal instinct of men and women.

I remember Vikram being a bit weak towards him from the very first day and since then he has easily joined the job. Although his educational qualifications are not low, it seems that he has become a P.S.

Moreover, Vikram does not give him less gifts for one night যে the famous Android mobile for his use is also a Rolex watch from last month given to him by Vikram.

He also promised to give a four-wheeler next month for his personal use! So to give yourself to Vikram - to open the veil - what is the fault?

But Vikram has a family, a wife and a child who has been detained for years, so sometimes the mood is a little bad, isn't it?

Isn't he separating Vikram from his family?
Manisha asks herself ...

Chapter Three

ButVikram does not like to give any kind of protection in bed. Better a poor horse than no horse at all.

At the first birthday party, that is, on the night of the first sexual intercourse with Vikram, there was no telling how many times she had sexual intercourse.

But what is there to fear? Besides, she had seen Binjanap on TV herself - so she bought a kid from a drug store without delay and checked it with her own hands - the report came back negative - she has not been caught in the trap of illegal pregnancy yet.

That started then Wherever Vikram Spent the night in Truro with বন taking a tablet Unwanted-72 in 72 hours If there is a problem then the pregnancy test kit is her place of trust.

Is it as if Manisha sat down with Vikram one day and said that you have a family - you have a wife and you have children and you have no guilt to have an illicit relationship with me?
Vikram said. What if Manisha - the food of the house can be eaten on a daily basis - it may be a balanced diet! But it's a big conventional thing - how do you eat panse panse - that's why people sometimes eat in hotels or restaurants ... isn't it?

It removes the monotony and makes the mind happy - that is the food of my hotel.
Listening to Vikram's argument, Manisha said in a haughty tone- And I understand only your hotel food?

If not you, my favorite dish is as balanced as it is full of nutrients - said Vikram ...

But Vikram is disgusted with meals at the hotel - so a family means a marriage ...
There is - there is a hundred times - there is no problem - we will be as we are if you say I can see a boy for you ...

O Hari, will you see a boy of honest character like you? Leaving his wife at home - will he have fun with PS at the hotel?

Of course, he is my advantage to the family and a big job… it may be foreign, but it works as a tonic in life - the body keeps the mind well, I was reading a survey ...

Survey of what?

Chapter Four

Thesurvey found that men and women who have sex at least three days a week have a longer life expectancy and increase their physical capacity.

That's right Will the Mahabharata become impure if you have a relationship with your married wife?

This cannot be explained to you Manisha ... you get married - in a few days you will understand everything.

Then you will see just dig around, all the love sounds will disappear ...

The reality will come down to the ground and it will be bloody to eat! Life will sway in the cradle of death - then you will find a window like mine - through which a little light - a little air a little pure oxygen to survive - a little colorful sky you will be desperate to find.
And if you find that window, you will want to grab it at any cost.

Although it is illegal in the eyes of foreign society, it is also in the eyes of law in our country It has been legal for the last two years. The Supreme Court's Division Clear Branch has ruled that adultery is not illegal. Permission or will is not a matter of coercion.

You see, as time goes on, it will become a socialism ... no one will bother about it anymore - like abroad.

But what will happen if everyone like you and me becomes intoxicated in the economic infrastructure of our country?

Yeah Al that sounds pretty crap to me, Looks like Manisha aint for me either ... The ones who have the will, the one who has the courage, but the one who doesn't have the financial well-being, it's going to take a deadly shape. To the power of Death can happen.

And you mean, like, saltines and their ilk, eh? In whose house the wife will spend the night with the man, and the husband will spend the honeymoon in the hotel with the other's wife.
Is this the real legitimacy of today's society ???

" Migratory"

Sincethere is no farming in the village in the country, there was scarcity of grain and food grains, so a couple of sparrows could take their baby with them in a different state ...

In the factory - sometimes in the garage or cleaning the streets, the day was going on a lot ... the children were also growing up in the fan-rice ...

In this way, many days and nights were spent happily.

At that time, the whole world was plagued by an unknown virus!

Lockdown in the air ... just a sound floating around ... Well do not eat this lockdown in the head?
Who knows
All the work around was learned - so stop eating ... Who knows where the house captivity ends?
The little ones in the house are gone ... How do you do that?

The sparrow couple, thinking that they can still survive by boiling vegetables and leaves in the country, started flying again with their strong will and courage. But how far is it possible to go this way?
With no water ... While flying, I suddenly saw a palace-proof house ...

In that house, there must be a lot of food arranged in the

stars, the eyes of the male bird became shining at the thought ...

Telling the rest of the members to wait for a while, the male bird flew straight to the palace - his guess is correct. Many are busy eating ... so he waited on the verandah, hoping to get some leftovers!

Seeing him, the slaves, the servants and the bakers all started a commotion.

The ascent is immediately followed by the fallen earth ... just like a worn out body How many days have I not had enough water in my stomach - so this misery of climbing ...

Slaves and nobles shouted that the sparrow was dead -
Disaster is what is left in the drain next to it ... The order of the owner of the palace is in a moment ...!

After noon, the climb did not return. The food was not enough. I saw the body of the bird ...
So seeing - two children suffering from hunger and thirst Fainted and did not respond to hundreds of calls ...
It is already evening!

Mother climbs lost direction… what will she do? Who is responsible for this situation?
Sitting in front of the lion door of the palace, mother Charai started crying loudly ...

The message reached Absolute Mars ...
A cloudburst of clouds began to form across the sky - As

if hundreds of thousands at once The mad elephant roared together and then began to sway!

After a while it started with the super cyclone Heavy rain with waste electricity ...
The whole city trembled and trembled and all was destroyed and sank into the abyss ...
Prasad Basirao then Tahi-Tahi Rob raised ... But salvation? No ...

This is how the whole city was flooded for a few days ... Death procession around!
The people of Prasad have taken shelter on the top floor - but the surprise is that they too have run out of water ... What will be the way now?

Mother is sitting on the top of the climbing pass and watching everything through the eyes of the stone.

Finished .....

PREFACE

There was a little girl
Who lived in another world
She read and wrote and pondered
Through fields and woods she wondered

She loved a good fairy tale
Her stories were her holy grail
She wanted to share her world
Ever since she was a little girl

So here is a small collection
For a little disconnection
Take a glimpse into this mind
I hope you enjoy whatever you find

Who do you think you are?

Almond eyes in a round face
My favourite colour is stretched across my skin
Spots like a leopard
A stranger in the mirror staring back at me
With the same eyes
Thick water proof skin allows the insults to roll
from my back
Like pouring tar down a hill
There's a tree farm on my trunks, growing at a
rate faster than happiness
My trunks rub together to create fire through
friction
Leaves burn between my thighs
Pain
Scars mark my body like a broken tapestry
A fungus grows across my canvas
Disgusting
Painful
Sad
What is this life
What is this thing that I see when I look at my
reflection
I don't know you
I don't know her
What is she?

A tub of fat encased in skin and muscle and
blood
Who do you think you are?

The Lonely Crow

A lone crow sat on a white fence, staring at a
barren field
And the crow called out for a friend to help ease
his loneliness.
In response, the sky gave him rain, hoping to
wash it away,
But no other crow came,
and so the crow called again
Once again the sky gave rain and once again no
crow came
For a full month, the crow called out and the sky
gave rain.
No crow came, but the barren field began to
grow green
And with each new green life that grew in the
field,
A new creature came to see,
So everyday the crow called, the sky gave rain
And a new creature came stay.

Jacaranda Jacaranda

Everywhere I go
The Jacarandas grow
And I think of that game you play

And I don't know when
I lost you friend
But I miss you every day

Those purple blooms
Will forever loom
In a place just for you

Despite the past
Our love will Last
Our friendship is deep and true

Inside my heart
You'll never part
No matter the space between

And I'll call you friend
Until the end
Even when you remain unseen.

My Grief

There's an ache in my chest
And some days it will rest
But some days I can't breathe
Through the pain of my grief

And the dread it grows
and it overflows
Until I can't see
And I can't let it be.

And the weight in my limbs
Fills everything
And I'm being pulled beneath
by the weight in my feet

And I'm drowning in sorrow
There is no tomorrow
I cannot wake
From this meaningless state.

Breathe, Breathe, Calm

Breathe,
In, Out, Breathe.

Let go of the weight in your heart

Breathe,
Out, in, again

Release your fears, let go of the anxiety.

Calm,
Two, three, four,

This is the best place to start.

Breathe,
Relax, just breathe

There is no dread on your chest

Breathe,
Think, Breathe again

This is not a nightmare

Calm,
Release, Let go

You're the one who knows you best

Breathe
It's okay, breathe

Don't let it overwhelm you

Breathe,
Be still, calm

You are the one with control

Calm
You're fine, breathe

This grief will fade too.

Smudge, Vinnie & Luna

A little black cat,
Sat on my lap
His Ginger haired brother beside him

They played with each other
And pestered their mother
Trying to escape outside again

Out through a hole
They found in a wall
And into the garden beyond

They ran and they played
Enjoying the day
As they climbed through the growing frond

And all the while
Quiet and docile
Their mother lay in the sun

Enjoying the heat
That warmed her feet
And watching her boys have fun

Whilst inside the house
Quiet as a mouse
I sat and watched them play

My three little cats
Who curl up in my lap
At the end of a playful day.

Baxter the Dog

There's a warm weight at my feet
As I fall into sleep, into dreams

And he's big and he's heavy
As he's getting ready to sleep

In his dreams he's always running

While awake never mean or cunning

And he cuddles against me
Always protecting my dreams.

Peacefulbay

I always know, when the warm wind blows
And sand dances around my feet
That there's magic out there, floating through
the air
And breathing life into me

When I feel down, or knocked around
I go to the place of my heart
Where the sand is fine, and the water sublime
As I wait for my healing to start

Never any fear, as I sit on the pier
And I watch as the waves come in
My feet in the water, the day getting hotter
And I slip in the ocean to swim

I can float in that pool, that endless blue
That always hold me a drift
And it fill my soul, fills that black hole
As I feel my spirits lift

And when it is done, the day has gone
The sun settles over the west
I go back home, to my Grandparents abode
Where I know I'm loved the best.

In the night

Deep in the night
I fear a fright
I fear the things I can't see

I hear a sound
It's all around
What is stalking me?

Can you hear?
It's barely clear
It whispers in my ear

The slightest brush
A gentle hush
I feel it passing near

The softest touch
It's all too much
My heart a beating drum

It brushed my knuckle
I hear a chuckle
When will the night be done

It's having fun
When it is done
A quivering mess I'll be

There's barely light
This deep in the night
With just my shadow and me.

Those Pieces

There are two sides to me
One I do not smother
This belongs to my father
Two sisters and a brother

And though I love both dearly
The other belongs to my mother
This here is a clear winner
There's my sister and my brother

It may not seem like it
My heart can be closed and cold
But those two pieces of my heart
I'll cherish until I'm old

I will never remove them
These pieces they belong
I can't imagine being without them
They've been with me all along

Those pieces of my mother
That live outside my heart
Those living, breathing memories
I hope they never part.

Darling Heart

The world is not an evil place,

My sweet girl

But bad things do happen

And although I've left you behind,

In the world

One day I'll see you again

Through every spin of the earth

Each day

And every turn around the sun

I'll be waiting until it's your turn

My love

Until your time is done

But until that long future time

Is here

Before you're ripe with age

I'll be guiding over your life

And loving you

Until I see you again.

Disconnect

There's silence where your voice should be
The messages remain unread
Activity on your account has gone silent
Your absence fills me with dread

I begin to forget what you look like,
I can't remember the sound of your voice
I think I'm beginning to forget you
It's not like you gave me a choice

Who told you, you could go?
Why did you have to leave me?
I really need to find you
I'll hunt you down, you'll see…

I'll look in all the places
I know you like to hide
And then when I find you
You'll be filled with pride

There's movement on the corner
I see you through the corner of my eye
The way you glance around
Your beauty I cannot deny

I always knew I'd find you
Now I can recall your face
I can recall your melodic voice
Thought you could disappear without a trace?

I will always come for you
I'll always be so near
I'll wait forever to be with you
There's nothing for you to fear

I can hear your footsteps approaching
Getting closer to my hiding place
I cannot wait to surprise you
To see that look on your face

I see that Horror in your eyes
The happiness is gone
But how could I have missed the knife
My love, what have you done?

I lay in my own misery,
As you stand and watch me die
But alas my love, I'll never leave you
I'll wait for you in the afterlife.

The Wind

The wind, the wind, it whispered a tune
and the tune sounded just like you

The Melody played through my head all day
And the colours around me were blue

They swirled through the air and swirled through
my hair
They filled my soul with a song

I got chills on my skin and I started to grin
And I felt you there all along.

A Stone

There's a stone in my shoe
It reminds me of you

It was barely there
But now I'm aware

It's all I can feel
Right there in my heel

It's digging in
Getting under my skin

I want it gone
But it's holding on

It perseveres
Through all my tears

It's dug in deep
I cannot sleep

It's always there
I'm always aware

Of this stone in my shoe
That reminds me of you.

Woman

Woman is a beautiful word
Perfectly rounded like a body
Slim and compact
Big, bold and embodied

Woman is a privilege
An honor to represent
Sexy and sweet
Strong and Independent

Vulnerable when needed
Strong when desired
Able to take control
Or give it up when required

Woman is incredible
No matter how you came to be
Whether you chose the privilege
Or were born to it, like me.

I'm sorry

I'm sorry I broke the plate
I'm sorry mum, I am

Please don't cry again, please
I'll fix it if I can

I didn't mean to make you cry
Or to make you sad

I'll clean it up, I promise mum
Please tell me you're not mad

I know sometimes you feel alone
With me always being away

In the hospital all the time
I miss you every day

The needles don't hurt anymore
I feel so healthy now

Maybe I can come home mum?
I just want to make you proud

I'm sorry if I hurt you,
But I just don't understand

Why won't you ever look at me
Please just hold my hand

Don't you want me anymore?
Did I do something wrong?

You never talk to me anymore
Mummy it's been too long

I heard you crying yesterday
Into daddies chest

You said "I can't believe she's gone"
He said "Our girl's at rest"

Please tell me the truth mummy,
Because I haven't gone away

I'll always be here for you
Each and every day

I'm sorry I couldn't hold on
I didn't mean to be too weak

And I couldn't say how much I love you
Because my mouth just wouldn't speak

I didn't mean to die mum
But mummy can't you see?

I'll always be here with you
Please say you still love me.
24

Autumn

A petal fell in my garden,
Then more petals followed in suit
The air is humid and the wind is warm
The trees have lost their fruit

The green has started dying
The pinks are now orange and brown
Leaves are leaving carpets
All over the dirty ground

The wind is causing a rustle
It smells of dying flora
Leaf piles are barely lasting
Making chao from the order

The sun is setting sooner
The night lasts a little longer
This is my favourite season
When the witching hour is stronger

Ghosts

There were ghosts wandering the night.
They haunt the halls of my life
They never try to frighten me
They aren't here out of spite

These lost souls were wanderers
The dreamers and the poets
The ones who chose to ponder
And live their lives to the fullest

Even now they're writing
They're coming up with dreams
They whisper them to me softly
My thoughts bursting at the seams

I write these thoughts on paper
I let them leave my head
And then that ghost moves on
And the next one moves ahead.

I was Raised by Witches

I was raised by women
Who were cunning and who were driven
Who loved their family wholly
And who raised them to be worthy

They had power in their bones
And that power fuelled their homes
Their properties were acres
Where they were the homemakers

And everyone who knew them
Knew they would be condemned
If they ever crossed the line
They would have to do the time

For these women and their power
These witches in their tower
Would set a curse upon you
If your goodness was not true

And I was raised to call my army
If someone threatened or alarmed me
And they would rise up fighting
For my family just knows one thing

You would never see a sun rise
Nor see beauty through your eyes
For these witches would make you suffer
For we know we are tougher.

We were raised by Witches
Who are cunning, beautiful bitches
And we would destroy the ground you walk on
If you ever were to hurt one

Gemini

I was born a Gemini
That fact has never changed
I have a flexible personality
Which is often re-arranged

My soul has different sides
Bits dark and some bits light
I can be meek and submissive
Or I can put up a fight

I have the kind and loving parts
That are always fun and happy
Then there is mean part of me
Who gets tired and often snappy

Sometimes I feel like two people
Are trapped inside my body
One is outrageous and courageous
The other alone and a homebody

My mother used call me
Her crazy Gemini
Because my personality
Would switch up on the fly

I know both these parts of me
I have accepted them whole hearted
It's not like they can ever leave
They are how I started.

The End

I used to think she would live forever

My mother, my best friend

But disease stole her away from me

Cancer took her in the end.

I used to think, she would always be here

That her gardens she would tend

She would nurture them forever

She would cultivate them till the end

I guess in a way she did that

She let her garden grow and bend

She left them to get over run

They went crazy in the end

I used to think, she was immortal

That her fire would never bend

I guess through her children she is

So she'll live forever in the end.